About this Book

KT-497-239

Murder on the Midnight Plane is a mystery story with a difference. The difference is that you have to solve the mystery yourself.

Throughout the book there are puzzles which you must solve in order for the next part to make sense. Clues and evidence are lurking in the words and the pictures.

Have a pencil and paper handy to help you work out the puzzles and to record your answers. You will need to use some of the answers and information from earlier pages to solve puzzles later in the book.

If you get stuck, there are extra clues to help you on page 41. These are printed in a special, cryptic way, so you will have to work out how to read them first. If you have to admit defeat, you will find the answers on pages 42 to 48.

Spike Sprockett

Sam Sprockett

The Sprockett twins are passengers on the midnight plane. They manage to find all the clues and solve the mystery. Now see if you can do the same.

3

At the Airport

The Sprockett twins, Sam and Spike, gazed down at the bustling confusion of Capitol City International Airport.

At last their holiday had begun and they were off to join their Uncle Tom in his search for buried treasure on Tsetse, one of the exotic Los Mosquitos islands.

Neither Spike nor Sam had ever flown in a plane before and they were both feeling more apprehensive than they dared to admit.

Spike looked at his watch. It was eight o'clock which meant their plane was due to leave in exactly one hour's time.

MURDER ON THE MIDNIGHT PLANE

Gaby Waters

Designed and illustrated by
Graham Round

Contents

"What do we do now?" asked Spike, hoping he sounded cooler than he felt.

"Go to the check-in desk of course," said Sam, trying to sound like an experienced air-traveller. "But I haven't a clue which one."

Spike sat on his case and stared through the railings. There were ten check-in desks.

"I think I know which one we want," he said. "Follow me."

DON'T TURN THE PAGE YET

Which check-in desk should they go to?

In the Departure Lounge

Half an hour later, the twins were slurping banana milkshakes in the departure lounge.

Spike was making gurgling noises with his straw, when he noticed someone standing beside him, reading a book about aeroplanes. Spike looked up and to his surprise, saw Barney, the boy who lived up the road.

"What are you doing here?" Spike spluttered.

Barney started to explain that he was off to Tsetse to see his granny, when an announcement boomed over the public address system.

"SWATAIR REGRET TO ANNOUNCE DELAYS OF THREE AND FOUR HOURS TO FLIGHTS SW 013 AND SW 015 RESPECTIVELY . . ."

There was a long wait ahead. Sam studied the strange collection of people in the departure lounge and listened. One by one she picked out the other passengers bound for Tsetse.

DON'T TURN THE PAGE YET

Which passengers are travelling to Tsetse?

That's our flight, Max. Now we're leaving at midnight.

How interesting . . . this book says that every plane which flies to Tsetse has just two propellers and carries up to 13 passengers.

Plane Spotting

It was nearly midnight. At last, their plane was ready for take-off. Sam and Spike ran along the maze-like corridors towards departure gate 13.

Suddenly, they found themselves in a long, dimly-lit room with an enormous window. They stopped to look out on to the floodlit tarmac below.

"I wonder which plane will take us to Tsetse," said Sam, thinking aloud.

Spike looked puzzled. He wished he had Barney's book of aeroplanes to look at, but Barney had run on ahead. Then he realized he could spot the plane without any extra help. In fact, it was really quite easy.

DON'T TURN THE PAGE YET

Which plane will Sam and Spike be travelling on?

8

On to the Plane

S am glanced at her watch. They were late! She grabbed Spike's arm, yanking him away from the window, and dashed down the corridor.

Suddenly, a man stepped out of nowhere. Sam crashed straight into him, spilling the entire contents of her bag over the floor.

The man muttered something under his breath. Then he bent down and started scooping Sam's possessions back into her bag.

Sam picked herself up and started to apologize, but the man had disappeared into thin air.

Sam snatched her bag and chased after Spike, through the departure gate and out on to the tarmac.

At last, they reached the plane. They clattered up the rickety steps and into the tiny cabin.

A stewardess stumbled towards them, took a flying leap over a pile of luggage and almost landed on Spike.

"Welcome aboard," she gasped, noting down the numbers of the twins' seats from their boarding passes.

She told them to go and sit in their seats, then she thrust a thick wad of leaflets into Spike's hands and disappeared.

The twins were bewildered. First, they had to find their seats but, judging by the chaos in the cabin, this was not an easy task. Spike searched for some seat numbers, but there did not appear to be any. He asked a man with a broken leg for some help, but the man was as puzzled as Spike. Then Sam had an amazing brainwave.

Seat Search

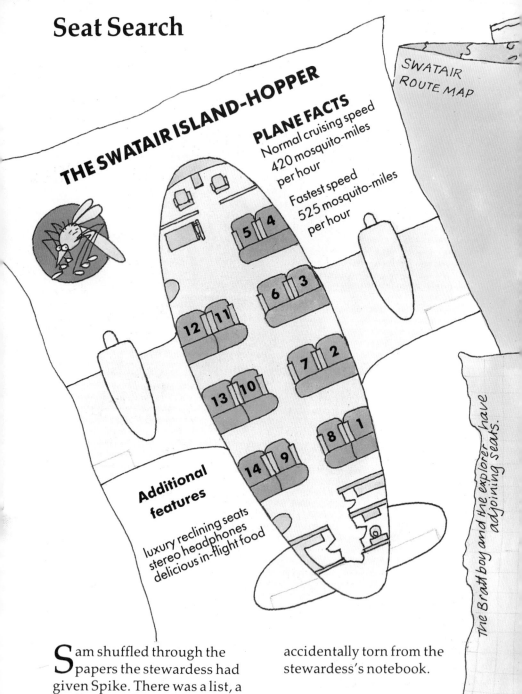

THE SWATAIR ISLAND-HOPPER

PLANE FACTS
Normal cruising speed
420 mosquito-miles
per hour

Fastest speed
525 mosquito-miles
per hour

Additional features

luxury reclining seats
stereo headphones
delicious in-flight food

SWATAIR
ROUTE MAP

The Bratt boy and the explorer have adjoining seats.

S am shuffled through the papers the stewardess had given Spike. There was a list, a plan, a map, a sick bag and even some handwritten notes, accidentally torn from the stewardess's notebook.

After a minute or two, Sam realized that she could easily

SWATAIR
PATENT
SICK BAG

Doctor Quickley sits behind
Billy Bratt

B.B.N. Pole has the
seat directly behind
Mr Megger-Bux

Ed Banger has multi-
coloured hair.

Sir Chand-Fyndes (and
his pet vulture) has an
aisle seat.

Mr & Mrs
Megger-Bux have
adjoining seats

PASSENGER LIST

PILOT   Charlie Sierra
CO-PILOT   Off sick
STEWARDESS   Dotty Fluster

Mr Max Megger-Bux
Mrs Megger-Bux
Mr Reeman
Barney B. N. Pole
Doctor Harry Quickley
Samantha Sprockett
Spike Sprockett
Pearl-Anne Plane
Christopher Wave
Sir Chand-Fyndes
Ed Banger
Billy Bratt
Inspector Ramsbottom

Mr Wave needs space for
his crutches—he has 2
adjoining seats in
the back row.

The doctor and the blonde
lady occupy adjoining seats.

Mr Reeman has seat
number 13.

No one sits in front
of Mrs Megger-Bux
(the pink haired
lady).

Ed Banger sits directly
in front of Mr Wave

Inspector Ramsbottom sits directly
behind Mrs Plane.

locate their seats. What was more,
she could work out where the
other passengers were sitting
and could even put names to
their faces.

DON'T TURN THE PAGE YET

**Can you match the names of the
passengers with their faces and
work out where each one sits?**

Death in the Air

A few hours later, the Tsetse plane was well on its way, flying due south, high above the Thalassic ocean.

Inside the plane, the passengers were pinned to their seats as the in-flight movie drew to a chilling and dramatic end.

Sam peered up the gangway to see the welcome sight of the stewardess wheeling out a clanking drinks trolley.

Almost everyone jumped to life at the sound of the drinks trolley. Spike leapt out of his seat and

fought his way through a jungle of grabbing hands, wobbling bottles and spilled drinks. At last,

he grabbed two glasses of cherrycola, only just saving them from the greedy grasp of Billy Bratt.

Spike was happily slurping his cherrycola when a bloodcurdling scream ripped through the plane.

The twins leapt up to find Barney looking very white and the man in front of Spike slumped half way across Barney's seat.

"Barney! What did you do to him?" yelled Sam.

"Nothing," Barney protested. "I just found him like this."

I'm a doctor.

Immediately, the man from seat number three dashed down the gangway clasping a big, blue bag.

He knelt over the man and examined him with all sorts of extraordinary medical instruments.

The doctor looked grim-faced. He stood up and exclaimed in a loud, serious voice, "This man is dead."

Was it the Food?

There was a stunned silence as the doctor laid a rug over the dead man.

"Wh...wh... what did he d..d..die of?" asked Barney, turning white.

"All the symptoms suggest food poisoning," said the doctor. "I strongly suspect that it was caused by something that the man ate for his dinner on this plane."

Spike turned a sickly shade of green as he thought back to the enormous food trolley laden with all sorts of delicious things.

Now he wished he hadn't been quite so greedy. He remembered every mouthful of gooey gateaux and greengage icecream. He could even recall everything the other passengers had eaten.

Then, in a flash of inspiration, Spike realized that he could easily use his memory to work out whether the doctor was right or not.

DON'T TURN THE PAGE YET

Was the dead man poisoned by the food he ate on the plane?

Spike Spots Something Suspicious

Spike announced his discovery in a loud voice, feeling a lot less green. Most of the other passengers seemed relieved, but the doctor just grunted and glowered at him.

All of a sudden, something caught his eye. He stared at it in horror. With a sickening jolt, he realized that if it WAS what it appeared to be, it cast an ominous shadow over the man's death.

What was more, Spike felt sure that he had seen it before. But where? He turned away for a split second. But when he looked back, it was gone. Had it disappeared or had someone hidden it?

DON'T TURN THE PAGE YET

These two pictures show what Spike saw before and after he looked away.

What was the suspicious thing Spike spotted?

AFTER

The Dead Man's Message

Spike wondered what to do next. Then he noticed the dead man's empty glass. He picked it up and sniffed it. Immediately, Spike knew there was something wrong.

"This tomato juice smells very strange," he said to the doctor.

But before the doctor could reply, the explorer, Sir Chand-Fyndes, pushed forwards and took the glass.

"A deceptive scent of strawberries," the explorer muttered, sniffing the glass. "This can only mean one thing . . . Akimbo poison! This man has been murdered."

There was a deathly hush. Then the man in the green overcoat walked down the gangway.

"I'm Inspector Ramsbottom," he said, flashing an identity card. "Tell me more about this poison."

"It comes from the deadly sap of the Akimbo tree," the explorer explained. "It smells sweet but kills instantly . . . and it always leaves a small ring of bright purple spots on the victim's face."

The explorer removed the dead man's hat and Sam gasped in horror. She recognized the dead man immediately.

Something in the back of her mind nagged her. Was she imagining it, or had he slipped an envelope into her bag?

Yes! There WAS an envelope! She tore it open and out fell a letter. It seemed to be written in a foreign language ... or was it?

Iha Vevita,

Lin forma ti onfory ourun cleconcer nin G.T. Hets et setre asuret "ELL-HIMT". Hata nanci entchar (TWH), ich pinpo int St. Hetre asur, eh? Asbe enst O'LENBY agre edygan gofbo. Un tyhun tersia, mont heirtra ilbu ticanno. Ti denti? Fyth emun ti lire acht set-sew. Heret hepro ofine edawa it smeth esetre ac: HEROUS VILLA,
IN-SARET,
RAVELLI, NGW.

I thus totset SETHEY WILLS to Patnot, hing TOPRO-TEC (TT). Heirsel (fish) plansan dife arfor myli feifa nyt, hin ghappen stomep. "LE ASEF" ol lowmyc luest heywi (LLL). Eady outot hecro, OK? Sandt hent othec hartt. He rearef urt herins tructi onsrol ledu pin-prin. T.T. Akeca re Andgo.

Odlu, **DON'T TURN THE PAGE YET**

C.K. **What does the letter say?**

Full Speed Ahead

There was no doubt that the dead man was telling the truth. His murder was the proof. Sam looked hard at the other passengers. Which ones were the crooks? Who was the murderer? If only she could find the answer. But no one looked remotely guilty.

Sam's thoughts were abruptly interrupted by the pilot's voice booming from a loudspeaker above her head.

"Owing to an unforeseen murder, we shall now fly at full speed, on the shortest course to Tsetse, in order to arrive ahead of schedule."

Sam glanced at her watch. It was half past three and they still had to find the dead man's further instructions. How much time did they have? She looked at the map the stewardess had given Spike.

"Where are we?" she muttered.

Just then, the stewardess waltzed by and told her. They were directly above the mouth of the River Okracoke.

DON'T TURN THE PAGE YET

How much time do Sam and Spike have left on the plane to find the further instructions?

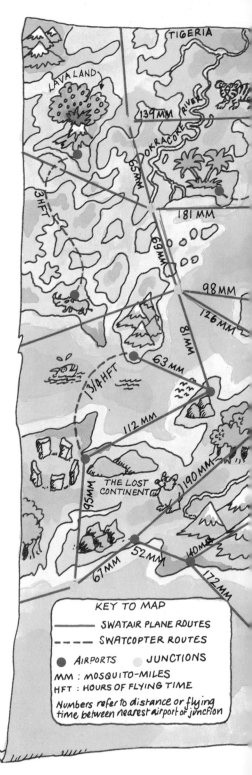

TIGERIA

LAVA LAND

139 MM

OKRACOKE RIVER

65 MM

3 HFT

181 MM

99 MM

98 MM

126 MM

81 MM

63 MM

1 3/4 HFT

112 MM

190 MM

95 MM

THE LOST CONTINENT

52 MM

67 MM

40 MM

172 MM

KEY TO MAP
——— SWATAIR PLANE ROUTES
- - - - SWATCOPTER ROUTES
● AIRPORTS ○ JUNCTIONS
MM : MOSQUITO-MILES
HFT : HOURS OF FLYING TIME
Numbers refer to distance or flying
time between nearest airport or junction

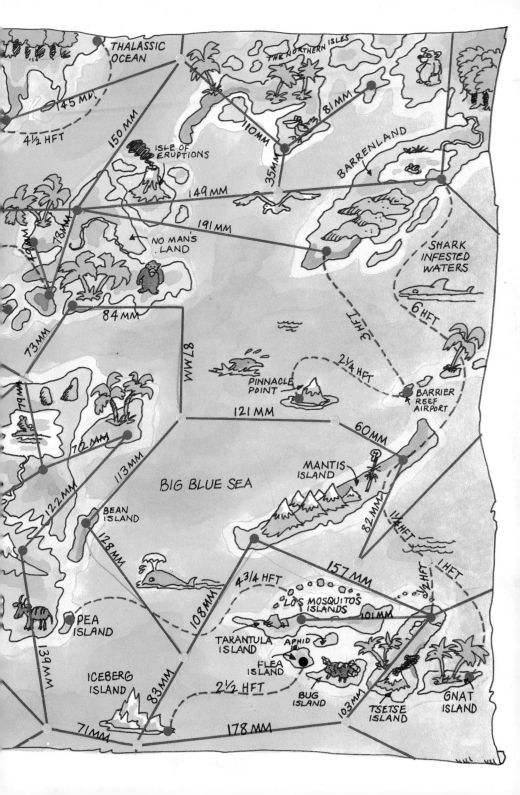

Chewy Toffees

The plane jolted into overdrive and began to climb. Immediately, Spike felt an alarming popping sensation inside his ears. Sam came up with a brilliant solution – an enormous box of chewy toffees. By now, everyone on the plane seemed to be complaining of ear popping, so Spike jumped up and passed them around.

Suddenly, something jolted his memory and he remembered where he had seen the poison bottle before. It had stood on the drinks trolley while everyone scrabbled for drinks and glasses.

How easy it must have been for the murderer to slip a few drops of poison into a glass of tomato juice. No one would have noticed, but Spike HAD noticed the hands around the trolley. What was more, he could remember each one very clearly.

If only he could work out whose hands they were, then he could draw up a list of murder suspects. In a flash of brilliance, Spike knew he could work it out. After passing round the toffees it was easy.

DON'T TURN THE PAGE YET

Who was at the drinks trolley?

Spike Finds the Poison Bottle

Spike slumped back down into his seat, feeling pleased with himself. Absent-mindedly, he dug his hand into the big box of chewy toffees and scrabbled around, feeling for his favourite flat, round ones.

All of a sudden, he felt something strange. It was cold and hard and not at all toffee-shaped. He looked down to investigate. He gasped when he saw it and a shiver ran down his spine. How had it dropped into the toffee box? There was only one way. The killer must have put it there while he was handing round the toffees.

He looked at the little bottle and hoped it hadn't leaked inside the toffee box. Then he realized that the poison bottle might actually lead him closer to the killer. He thought hard for a few minutes while a theory started to take shape in his mind. If he was correct, then he could narrow down the list of murder suspects even further.

DON'T LOOK AT THE OPPOSITE PAGE YET

How does Spike narrow down the list of suspects?
Which passengers are murder suspects?

Now spike was feeling extremely pleased with himself. He even started to wonder whether the Department of Criminal Investigation might offer him a holiday job.

He was roused from his day dream by the noise from the seat in front, where Inspector Ramsbottom was sorting through the dead man's possessions. Mrs Plane was helping the Inspector. Spike noticed that she seemed very interested in the dead man's things, but he could not decide whether this was suspicious or not.

Sam peered over the top of her seat. All at once, she remembered something, but she wasn't sure quite what it was. It niggled in the back of her brain and the more she stared at the man's things, the more the niggle grew.

Then she remembered the dead man's message and everything clicked into place. Of course! Now she knew where to find the dead man's further instructions.

DON'T TURN THE PAGE YET

Where are the dead man's further instructions?

A Message in the News

MYSTERY BANK BREAK-IN

by Horace Grovell

Police are investigating a mysterious break-in at Grimbleys Bank in London.

Last Friday night, crafty thieves outwitted the bank's highly sophisticated alarm system and penetrated the steel-walled underground vaults.

Until now, the bank's computerized system of hi-security, combination locks was believed to be foolproof. Specialists assisting the police say they are stumped. So far, they have been unable to work out how the cunning crooks broke through the intricate locking system and they have no idea how the alarm mechanism was discovered and temporarily de-activated.

But the thieves were unaware of an automatic

Grimbleys Bank: the police are stumped.

security camera, hidden in the wall of the vaults. A roll of film clearly shows the three villains inside the vault, but so far, the Police have been unable to identify them. The film has now been sent to Tsetse in the hope that someone on the island will recognize the crooks.

What makes this case so perplexing, is that nothing of any value was stolen. Bank officials report that the vault contains countless precious jewels and bank notes to the sum of many

millions. But just one safe-box was opened and this contained an apparently worthless roll of parchment.

The latest news from London is that the Police have handed the case over to a mystery man, believed to be a top private detective. This mystery man is said to have his own special theory concerning the theft. When questioned, he refused to comment, saying only that it was too dangerous to divulge his discoveries while the crooks were still at large.

Unexpected security leaks at Police HQ reveal that the mystery detective is linking the Grimbley's Bank robbery with the Tsetse treasure expedition, currently headed by Thomas Sprockett in the Los Mosquitos islands. There is a suggestion that the stolen parchment is an ancient treasure chart.

Spike waited for the Inspector to look the other way, then he stretched over and took the newspaper from the seat in front.

He wasn't sure quite what to look for. He opened it and started to read. Where were the dead man's instructions? At first he wasn't

PRICELESS IDOL DISCOVERED

A fantastic, gold statue has been unearthed in Egypt. Experts believe it to be the legendary "lost idol", buried thousands of years ago under the desert sands. More news on this fabulous find in tomorrow's edition.

Singer vanishes

ED BANGER, the ex-lead singer of "Awful Noises", disappeared from his New York apartment last Thursday. He has not been seen since.

Schoolgirl's solo stunts

CHLOE, the schoolgirl stunt pilot has broken another breathtaking record in the history of aviation, by flying solo from London to Toronto in just under 12 hours.

Speedy Nik

AMATEUR SKIING ACE, Speedy Nik, astounded spectators in a death-defying downhill race in Val Despair last Saturday. On his tungsten-tipped, three metre skis, Speedy zipped through deep gulleys of powder snow and cleared a bottomless crevasse with a staggering triple-twist back-flip to pip every contestant to the post. With this victory behind him, Speedy Nik is now talking of taking up water sports.

MILLIONAIRE

MULTIMILLIONAIRE, Maximillian Megger-Bux has denied rumours that he is fleeing the country to escape the fraud squad. He was spotted yesterday making two flight reservations to an undisclosed destination. Mr Megger-Bux claims he is simply taking a short vacation in the sun.

CLASSIFIED ADS

TEA LADY required. Apply to Boris Blood, Blood Castle, San Guinaria.

WANTED: Rare books on magic and ancient curses. Write to Drusilla P. Culia. P.O. Box 666.

FOR SALE: One ostrich outfit (with feathers). Miss Putty, Tel. 675 3018.

AMAZING DUNGEON SALE. Bargain spears, handmade rat traps and much much more . . . One day only! Friday 13th, Blood Castle.

FOR SALE: Custom built, triple-fin surf board with velcro ankle-strap. Christopher Wave, 1001 Ocean Boulevard, LA.

HAIR transplant urgently needed by embarrassed school master. Genuine offers only. Tel. 243276

sure, but the more he looked, the more obvious it became that the dead man was trying to tell them something.

DON'T TURN THE PAGE YET

What are the dead man's instructions?

Searching the Plane

S am and Spike were stumped. They had to find the dead man's vital information in order to hand it to Uncle Tom. But where were they supposed to start searching?

There was only one solution. Trying hard not to appear too inquisitive or suspicious, they searched every part of the plane from the galley through to the cockpit.

Half an hour later, they were almost on the point of giving up the search. Then they suddenly spotted it. Nobody noticed as Sam slipped it into the pocket of her dungarees.

DON'T TURN THE PAGE YET

These pictures show some of the places Sam and Spike searched. Where is the vital information?

The Landing Game

Now there was only one thing left to puzzle out. But what had the dead man meant by the "final trivial answer"? Was it a cryptic clue or even some sort of code? Spike racked his brains for inspiration and stared out of the window. With a sinking feeling, he realized they were starting their descent to Tsetse.

Sam peered round the back of Barney's seat. The stewardess was stumbling down the gangway, stopping at every row. At last she came to Sam and Spike.

"We're coming in to land now," she chirped, brightly. "I'm afraid it's going to be a very bumpy landing – it usually is with Captain Sierra at the joystick."

Spike started to feel nervous, but he hoped it didn't show. Then the stewardess handed him a card.

"Perhaps you would like to play the landing game," she said, trying to dispel Spike's obvious fears. "It might take your mind off the bumps."

Spike grimaced. Neither he nor Sam were in the mood for games, but he took the game card anyway. Sam glanced at it. Then she read the words printed at the top...

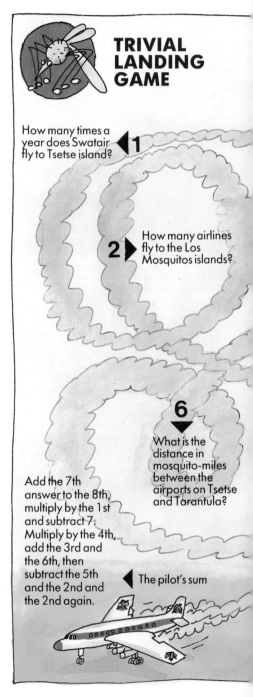

TRIVIAL LANDING GAME

1 How many times a year does Swatair fly to Tsetse island?

2 How many airlines fly to the Los Mosquitos islands?

6 What is the distance in mosquito-miles between the airports on Tsetse and Tarantula?

Add the 7th answer to the 8th, multiply by the 1st and subtract 7. Multiply by the 4th, add the 3rd and the 6th, then subtract the 5th and the 2nd and the 2nd again.

The pilot's sum

Find the final trivial answer and you stand to win a fabulous free flight of a lifetime.

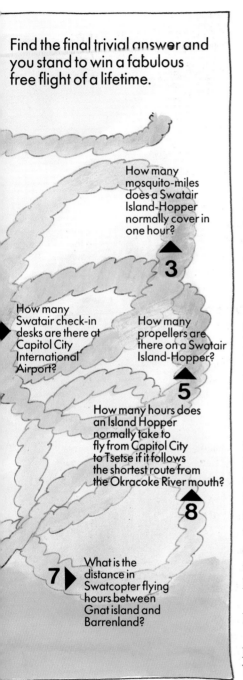

How many mosquito-miles does a Swatair Island-Hopper normally cover in one hour?

3

How many Swatair check-in desks are there at Capitol City International Airport?

How many propellers are there on a Swatair Island-Hopper?

5

How many hours does an Island Hopper normally take to fly from Capitol City to Tsetse if it follows the shortest route from the Okracoke River mouth?

8

7 ▶ What is the distance in Swatcopter flying hours between Gnat island and Barrenland?

"This is it!" she cried. "Quick! There's no time to lose."

"But how do we play this game?" asked Spike, searching for non-existent instructions.

The stewardess came to their rescue and explained.

"Follow the plane as it loops the loop towards the ground. Answer each question in turn, then work out the pilot's sum to find the final answer."

The twins worked quickly, using Spike's calculator and a lot of brain-power. Several minutes later, just as the landing wheels bounced on to the tarmac, the twins came up with the final answer.

Sam grinned from ear to ear as the plane taxied to halt. She leaned across and stared out of the window. Outside, she saw the tiny airport building and there, in the window, was Uncle Tom waiting for them. The twins leapt out of their seats in a scramble for the door and stepped out into the hot Tsetse sunshine.

DON'T TURN THE PAGE YET

**Play the landing game.
What is the final answer?**

A Perplexing Riddle

The twins threw themselves into Uncle Tom's arms and poured out the story of their flight. Then Sam thrust the yellow envelope into Uncle Tom's hands. He ripped it open and pulled out a piece of paper. On it was written a perplexing message and a riddle. At first it made no sense at all, but with a little inspiration, Uncle Tom and the twins puzzled out its meaning.

DON'T TURN THE PAGE YET

What is the meaning of this strange message?

The proof you need is waiting at the airport inside the answer to this riddle:

MY FIRST IS IN FLYING BUT NEVER AT NIGHT
MY SECOND'S IN PILOT BUT NEVER IN FLIGHT
MY THIRD'S NOT IN TREASURE BUT IS IN THE CHART
MY FOURTH IS IN TICKET BUT NOT IN DEPART
MY FIFTH IS IN DANGER AND ALSO IN RED
MY SIXTH IS IN MURDER BUT NEVER IN DEAD

Its number is the same as my seat. I have already given you the key that will open its door.

Proof in the Negatives

Inside the locker was yet another, bigger, yellow envelope. Uncle Tom unsealed it very carefully and gently lifted out two long strips of film. They were black and white negatives. He held them up to the light and stared at them.

"My goodness!" Uncle Tom exclaimed. "This film was taken in the vaults of Grimbleys bank. It actually shows the theft of the ancient treasure chart. It must have been taken by the bank's hidden automatic security camera."

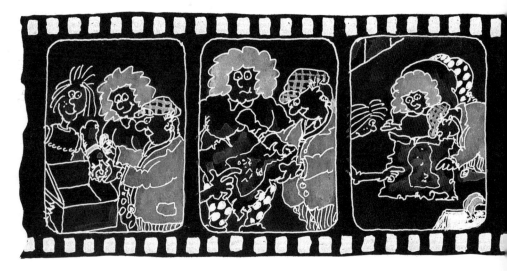

He held up the film to let Spike and Sam have a good look. It was hard to work out what was what as dark areas were shown as light and vice versa.

"Do you recognize these criminals?" asked Uncle Tom.

"Yes, I do," cried Spike, triumphantly. "And I know where to find the treasure chart, too!"

DON'T TURN THE PAGE YET

Who are the thieves and where is the treasure chart?

The Ancient Treasure Chart

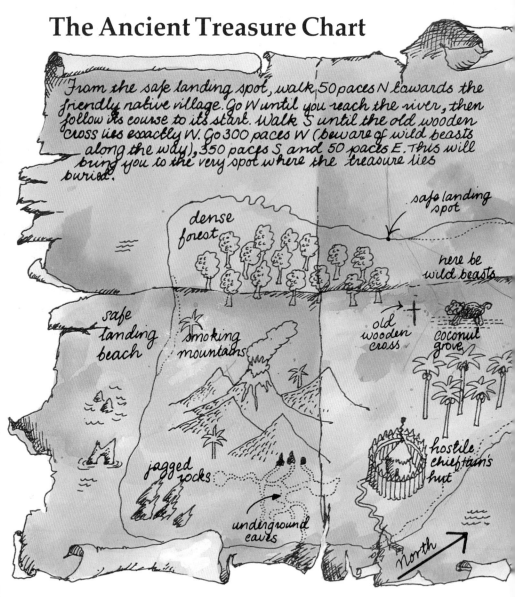

From the safe landing spot, walk 50 paces N towards the friendly native village. Go W until you reach the river, then follow its course to its start. Walk S until the old wooden cross lies exactly W. Go 300 paces W (beware of wild beasts along the way), 350 paces S and 50 paces E. This will bring you to the very spot where the treasure lies buried.

safe landing spot

dense forest

here be wild beasts

safe landing beach

smoking mountains

old wooden cross

coconut grove

jagged rocks

underground caves

hostile chieftain's hut

North

Uncle Tom dashed off in search of Inspector Ramsbottom. He left Sam and Spike sitting on a bench, crossing their fingers in the hope that the crooks hadn't made a quick getaway.

After what felt like hours, Uncle Tom returned with the Inspector. The crooks had been detained and the treasure chart rescued. Very cautiously, Uncle Tom unrolled the ancient, flaking map.

this line is the distance of 200 paces

HMS 'Honora' ran aground here 1698

Beware the quicksand

Coral reef

sinister statues

Malaria River

foul smelling swamp

Village (friendly natives)

here be dragons?

safe landing spot

galleon wrecked in storm Dec 1706

In the top left-hand corner there were some strange instructions written in ancient, spidery script. What did they mean? Then Sam had an idea and pulled out her little traveller's compass.

"I know how to find the treasure," she said.

DON'T TURN THE PAGE YET

Where is the treasure buried?

Naming the Killer

Uncle Tom rolled up the map and turned to the twins.

"Whatever would have happened if you hadn't travelled on the midnight plane?" he said. "Without you two, the Tsetse treasure would have been swiped by that bunch of unscrupulous bounty-hunters . . ."

"And they may never have been caught," added the detective.

Sam blushed. Then she remembered the poor man in seat number 13. Without him, they would never have been able to catch the crooks. But he was dead.

"But we still don't know who killed poor Mr Reeman," she said in a quiet voice.

Everyone was silent. Spike thought back. He remembered the drinks trolley . . . the box of sweets . . . the little poison bottle . . . and his list of murder suspects. Slowly, the facts started to fall into place.

"But we DO know who killed him," said Spike, feeling a bit more cheerful. "It's obvious!"

DON'T TURN THE PAGE YET

Who was the killer?

40

Clues

Page 4

Have you seen the adverts on the wall? The departure times are shown using the 24 hour clock.

Page 6

Look at the flight numbers on luggage labels and boarding passes. Pay special attention to what people are saying.

Page 8

Look for the airline logo and remember what Barney said on page 6.

Page 12

The most important clues are in the stewardess's notes. Go through each clue, one by one, working out where each passenger can and cannot possibly sit.
Look on pages 6-7 to find out some of the passenger's names.
Look on page 11 to find the numbers of Sam and Spike's seats.

Page 16

Did any of the passengers eat the same things as the dead man?

Page 18

This is easy. Use your eyes.

Page 20

Ignore spaces and punctuation marks.

Page 22

Look at the plane facts on page 12. Divide the speed of the plane per minute by the distance of the shortest route to Tsetse.

Page 24

Look carefully at the hands around the drinks trolley on page 14.

Page 26

If the killer dropped the poison bottle into the box, the killer must have been one of the passengers who accepted a toffee.

Page 27

Look back to the dead man's message on page 21. Where will the twins find further instructions?

Page 28

Have you noticed the dots on the newsprint?

Page 30

The message in the newspaper tells you what to look for. Use your eyes.

Page 32

You will need to flick back through the book to find some of the answers.

Page 34

The answer to the riddle is a six letter word. Each line of the riddle gives you a clue to a letter, in the correct order. Look at the newspaper message on pages 28-29 to find the key.

Page 36

The three thieves are passengers on the plane. Look carefully at their shapes, features and hands.

Page 38

N = North, S = South, E = East, W = West.
Where is North on the map?

Page 40

Which of the thieves are on the list of murder suspects?

Answers

Pages 4-5

Sam and Spike should go to check-in desk number 8. They are flying to Tsetse on flight number SW013 at 21.00 hours (9 o'clock).

Pages 6-7

The passengers travelling to Tsetse are ringed in black. Ignore the letters for now. They are part of the answer to the puzzle on pages 12-13.

Pages 8-9

The plane that Sam and Spike will be travelling on is ringed in black. It is the only SWATAIR plane which fits Barney's description of planes that fly to Tsetse (see page 6).

Pages 12-13

Here are the names and seat numbers of each passenger. Look over the page to fit the names with the faces.

Christopher Wave	1 and 8
Ed Banger	2
Doctor Harry Quickley	3
Billy Bratt	4
Sir Chand-Fyndes	5
Pearl-Anne Plane	6
Inspector Ramsbottom	7
Sam Sprockett	9
Barney B.N. Pole	10
Mr Megger-Bux	11
Mrs Megger-Bux	12
Mr Reeman	13
Spike Sprockett	14

To fit the names of the passengers with their faces, look at the picture on page 42. Match the letters beside each passenger with the letters beside each name in the list below. For instance, passenger A is Christopher Wave, passenger B is Ed Banger etc.

A	Christopher Wave	**H**	Sam Sprockett
B	Ed Banger	**I**	Barney B.N. Pole
C	Doctor Harry Quickley	**J**	Mr Megger-Bux
D	Billy Bratt	**K**	Mrs Megger-Bux
E	Sir Chand-Fyndes	**L**	Mr Reeman
F	Pearl-Anne Plane	**M**	Spike Sprockett
G	Inspector Ramsbottom		

Pages 16-17

Every item of food eaten by the dead man was also eaten by at least one other passenger. Since all the other passengers are alive and well, it is unlikely that the dead man was poisoned by his food.

Pages 18-19

Spike spotted a small bottle filled with green liquid. The skull and crossbones on the label suggest the liquid is poison.

When he looked again, the bottle was covered by Pearl-Anne Plane's knitting bag.

Pages 20-21

Sam and Spike decoded the message by removing all the spaces and punctuation marks. From the meaning of the message, they were able to insert new ones.

The decoded message reads as follows:

I have vital information for your uncle concerning the Tsetse treasure. Tell him that an ancient chart, which pin-points the treasure, has been stolen by a greedy gang of bounty hunters. I am on their trail but I cannot identify them until I reach Tsetse, where the proof I need awaits me. These treacherous villains are travelling with us to Tsetse. They will stop at nothing to protect their selfish plans, and I fear for my life. If anything happens to me, please follow my clues. They will lead you to the crooks and then to the chart. There are further instructions rolled up in print. Take care and good luck.

Pages 22-23

The shortest route to Tsetse is shown below, in black. It is 945 mosquito-miles long. The fastest speed of the plane is 525 mosquito-miles per hour (see page 12). If the plane flies at this speed all the way,

Sam and Spike have one hour and 48 minutes (108) minutes to find the dead man's further instructions. (This means they will arrive in Tsetse at 18 minutes past five.)

The plane is here

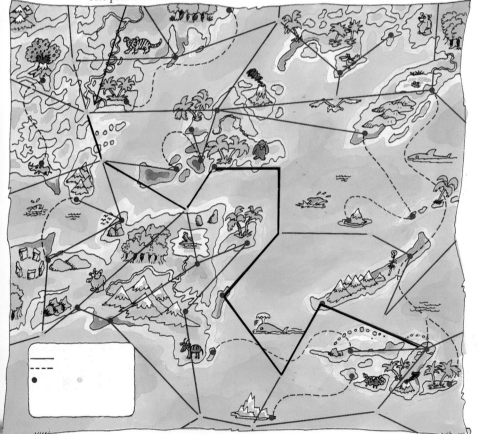

Here you can see who was standing at the drinks trolley. Any one of these people (except for the dead man) could be the murderer.

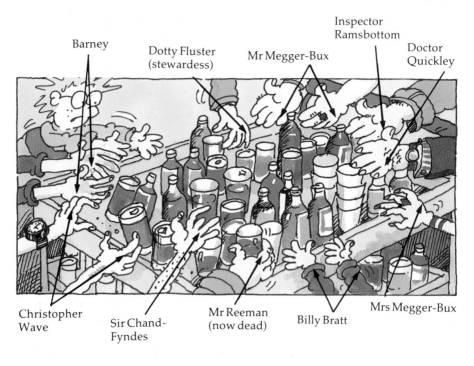

Barney

Dotty Fluster (stewardess)

Mr Megger-Bux

Inspector Ramsbottom

Doctor Quickley

Christopher Wave

Sir Chand-Fyndes

Mr Reeman (now dead)

Billy Bratt

Mrs Megger-Bux

Page 26

Spike realizes that if the killer dropped the poison bottle into the toffees, then the killer must have been one of the people who accepted a toffee. Those who refused did not put their hands into the toffee box (see pages 24-25).

Four people refused a toffee: Inspector Ramsbottom, Pearl-Anne Plane, Mrs Megger-Bux and Barney. They are struck off the list of murder suspects, leaving Christopher Wave, Doctor Quickley, Billy Bratt, Sir Chand-Fyndes, Mr Megger-Bux and Dotty Fluster, the stewardess.

Page 27

The dead man's instructions are in the rolled-up newspaper. Sam realized this when she remembered this sentence in his message:
   "There are further instructions rolled up in print."

Pages 28-29

To decipher the dead man's instructions, take the letters with dots beneath them and put them together, in order. This is what they say:

Vital information is hidden on this plane inside a yellow envelope. Find it and give it to your uncle. The final trivial answer is the key that will open the door.

Pages 30-31

From the newspaper message on pages 28-29, the twins know that the vital information is in a yellow envelope. This is hidden in the vulture's cage.

Pages 32-33

The answers to the trivial questions are shown below.

1	52	5	2	Final answer
2	1	6	101	
3	420	7	8.25 (8¼)	1959
4	2	8	5.75 (5¾)	

Pages 34-35

The answer to the riddle is the word LOCKER. The strange message tells Uncle Tom and the twins that they will find the proof they need in a (baggage) locker at the airport. The locker number is 13 (the same as the dead man's seat). The "key" to open the locker is the number 1959 which is the final answer to the trivial landing game (see pages 32-33). The twins know this from the newspaper message on pages 28-29.

Baggage locker number 13.

Pages 36-37

The thieves are Doctor Quickley, Pearl-Anne Plane and Ed Banger. The ancient treasure chart is in the Doctor's bag.

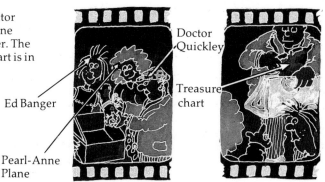

Doctor Quickley

Ed Banger

Treasure chart

Pearl-Anne Plane

Pages 38-39

X marks the spot where the treasure is buried. The black line shows the course that Sam plotted to discover this.

Page 40

In his first message (see pages 20-21), the dead man reveals his life is in danger from the thieves. But only one of them murdered him. Neither Pearl-Anne Plane nor Ed Banger was at the drinks trolley when the poison was added to the dead man's drink, which means that Doctor Quickley was the killer.

First published in 1986 by Usborne Publishing Ltd, 20 Garrick Street, London WC2E 9BJ, England.

Copyright 1986 Usborne Publishing Ltd.

The name Usborne and the device are Trade Marks of Usborne Publishing Ltd.

Printed in Belgium.